TWO CRAFTY JACKALS

ALSO BY ELIZABETH LAIRD

The Lure of the Honey Bird: The Storytellers of Ethiopia (2013)

Shahnameh: The Persian Book of Kings (2012)

The Prince Who Walked with Lions (2012)

The Ogress and the Snake and Other Stories from Somalia (2009)

Pea Boy and Other Stories from Iran (2009)

A Fistful of Pearls and Other Tales from Iraq (2008)

Lost Riders (2008)

Crusade (2007)

Oranges in No Man's Land (2006)

The Garbage King (2003)

A Little Piece of Ground (2003)

When the World Began: Stories Collected in Ethiopia (2000)

Kiss the Dust (1991)

Red Sky in the Morning (1988)

Two CRAFTY JACKALS

The ANIMAL FABLES of KALILAH and DIMNAH

ELIZABETH LAIRD

Illustrations Attributed to SADIQI BEG

AGA KHAN MUSEUM

CONTENTS

INTRODUCTION

A good story is like a river. It starts from far away and travels on and on, passing through one country after another, bringing life and pleasure along its way.

The stories in this book began their lives in India more than two thousand years ago, and they have been travelling ever since. They passed through the ancient languages of Sanskrit, Pahlavi, and Syriac and were already a thousand years old when they were translated into Arabic. They jumped from Arabic into Persian, and then they continued travelling. They went back to India and then to Afghanistan and Georgia and Turkey. Later they arrived in Europe and were translated into Spanish and Italian and German and French and English and many other languages.

These lovely stories, all wrapped up in one another so that sometimes one begins before the last has ended, tell the tale of Dimnah, a crafty little jackal who sets out to get the better of the mighty King of Lions, and Dimnah's brother, Kalilah, who tries to stop him from making too many mistakes.

All the way through the history of these stories, great artists have been inspired to illustrate them. The pictures in this book have been attributed to the Iranian artist Sadiqi Beg, who lived more than four hundred years ago. If you go to the Aga Khan Museum in Toronto, Canada, you can see for yourself the original paintings in the manuscript. You will find they are as fresh and beautiful as ever.

8

nce there was a great Shah who ruled over many lands. He wanted above all things to be wise so that his nation would live in peace and his people would be happy.

The Shah knew that wherever there is a powerful person there are others who are jealous. And when people are jealous they can be tempted to spread unkind rumours. They can be deceitful and destructive.

"I need to be on my guard against those who might try to hurt me," the Shah said to his best friend and counsellor. "Can you give me some advice?"

The counsellor thought for a while, then said, "Let me tell you a story. It's about a lion, a bull, and two crafty little jackals."

The Shah smiled and lay back comfortably on his cushions. "I like stories. Go on."

9

There was once a merchant who travelled about from town to town. His goods were loaded on a heavy cart, which was pulled by two strong bulls.

As they went along, one of the bulls, whose name was Shanzabeh, fell into a swamp. The merchant and his servants tried to pull him out, but poor Shanzabeh was stuck fast in the mud.

"We'll have to leave you here," the merchant said at last. "You'll be able to climb out when the mud dries up."

Then off he went with his servants and the other bull.

After a while Shanzabeh found that he could scramble out of the swamp. He wandered about until he came to a meadow of lush grass dotted with exquisite flowers through which ran a stream of cool, clear water. Shanzabeh, who was very hungry and thirsty, ate and drank his fill, then lifted his head and bellowed with joy, delighting in his newfound freedom until his echoes rang from the hills all around.

Not far away was the domain of a mighty lion. He ruled like a king over all the other animals, who followed him about, flattering him and fawning over him.

The Lion, strutting with proud disdain,
Patrols the borders of his domain.
There is nothing he dreads, no one he fears.
His subjects tremble when he appears.

The King of Lions had never been afraid in his life, but he had never heard the roaring of a bull, and Shanzabeh's bellowing terrified him. He didn't even dare to march around his borders in the way he had done before, but stayed fixed in one place.

Two crafty jackals hung about the court of the King. One was called Kalilah and the other's name was Dimnah. Both of them were clever and quick-witted, but Dimnah was greedy and ambitious, too.

"Have you noticed, brother," asked Dimnah, "that our lord the King never moves about anymore? He used to roam around the country, but now he hardly stirs himself."

"The King can do as he pleases," answered Kalilah. "It has nothing to do with us. We're of no importance to him. He looks after us, and that should be enough. Anyway, it's dangerous to poke your nose into the affairs of your betters."

Dimnah shook his head. "I'm tired of being a nobody, lurking on the edge of the court, being ignored by all the important animals. I want to get close to the King and become his friend and adviser."

"And how will you do that?" asked Kalilah scornfully.

"Don't you see?" said Dimnah. "This is my chance. Something has upset and disturbed the King. If I can find out what it is, I may be able to help him."

"But you're only a little jackal!" said Kalilah. "You're not like those grand creatures who surround our lord and master."

شوكت وحوش بسيار دردخدمت اوكوهيند
وسباع بشمار سهمتابعت برحظ ذهان

اوهاده شير از عزوجوانى ونخوت حكومت
وكامرانى وكثرت خدم وبسياري حشم كسى

"Maybe not," said Dimnah, "but if he does come to favour me, I'd serve him well. I'd be sincere and loyal and give him the best advice."

"Well, if you really want to try your luck," said Kalilah, "you'd better take care. Being close to a powerful king is like being close to a fire. Your whiskers might burn and your fur might be singed. Still, if you're determined, I wish you the best of luck."

So Dimnah brushed his tail and polished his claws and crept up to the King of Lions, bowing low.

"Who is this?" asked the King, turning his noble head and staring down at Dimnah.

"I'm Dimnah the jackal, and I'm the lowest of all your creatures."

"Hmm," said the King. "I suppose I'd better have a look at you. Come here, little jackal. What do you want?"

Dimnah took a deep breath. "Your Majesty, you're surrounded by noble lords, and I'm only small and unimportant, but my wits are quick, and sometimes the advice of a humble person can be useful to a King."

The nimble fly darts to and fro,
Watching all who come and go,
While on the ground the gaudy peacocks glide,
Shaking their tails in all-consuming pride.

"I'm like that little fly, O King. I see and hear everything, and I can tell Your Majesty what's really going on, unlike those puffed-up nobles in your court."

The King's courtiers were none too pleased to hear this, but the King smiled. "That's good. I can see you're a clever fellow. I need counsellors like you. We'll talk again."

Dimnah was delighted by his success, and from that moment on he spent all his time close to the King, who came to trust him and treat him as a friend.

One day, when they were alone together, Dimnah said to the King, "I can see that something troubles you, sire. You used to patrol your borders, but now you remain in one spot. May I know the reason?"

آورده اند که روباهی در بیشه‌ای می‌رفت و بوی طعمه هر طرف می‌کشت پای درختی

رسید که طبلی از پهلوی او آویخته بودند

وهرگاه که بادی وزیدی شاخی ازان

درخت در حرکت آمده بروی طبل رسیدی و آوازی سهمگین ازوی برآمدی روباه

The King was ashamed to admit that he was scared of nothing more than the strange bellowing he could hear.

"Nothing troubles me," he said with a royal frown, but at that very moment Shanzabeh the bull roared so loudly that the ground shook under Dimnah's feet. The King trembled violently. "That dreadful din! It terrifies me! Whoever roars like that must be the mightiest and most ferocious of creatures."

Dimnah's heart leaped with joy. At last he had discovered the King's secret. Now he began to think how he could turn it to his advantage. "Your Majesty is too great a king to be worried by a mere sound. It might just be an empty noise. After all, think about what happened to the fox."

"What fox?" asked the King.

"I'll tell you," said Dimnah.

The STORY of the FOX and the DRUM

Once there was a fox, who was always hunting for something to eat. For a long time he had no luck and grew hungrier and hungrier until at last he caught sight of a plump little chicken pecking by the roots of a tree.

The fox crept up to the tree but did not realize that a drum had been hung overhead and was hidden among the leaves. Just as he crouched, ready to pounce, a gust of wind knocked the branches of the tree against the drum.

Da-da-boum! went the drum. *Da-da-boum!*

The fox looked up.

"Such a loud noise must be coming from a really big animal," he said to himself. "It'll make a better meal than this scrawny little chicken."

So he scrambled up the tree and attacked the drum. All he found, of course, was some skin and pieces of wood. Disappointed, he jumped down again.

Now where's that chicken? he thought. *I'll have to make do with it, after all.*

But the chicken had wisely scurried away.

"That's all very well," said the King when Dimnah finished his story, "but I still don't know what's making that terrible noise. It might not be anything as harmless as a drum."

"I'll go and find out," said Dimnah.

Off he trotted, and soon he came upon Shanzabeh, who was happily grazing in the meadow.

"I have a message for you from the lion, the King of the Beasts," Dimnah said importantly. "He has ordered you to approach him and pay your respects. He will only forgive you for not coming to him earlier if you follow me at once."

Shanzabeh was frightened when he heard this. "The K-king of L-lions?" he stammered. "But if I go to him he might tear me to pieces."

"I'll protect you," said Dimnah grandly. "You can rely on me."

And so, stepping timidly on his shiny black hooves, Shanzabeh approached the King. The lion was so relieved to see an ordinary animal, rather than the monster he had been imagining, that he took a liking to Shanzabeh straight away, and soon he and the bull were the best of friends. From now on it was Shanzabeh the bull to whom the King turned for advice, while Dimnah was ignored. It was Shanzabeh's wisdom that the King relied on, while Dimnah was left out in the cold.

> *Envy and hatred now conspire*
> *To light in Dimnah's heart a raging fire.*

Dimnah, mad with jealousy, went to see Kalilah.

"I'm sorry for you, dear brother," said Kalilah, "but I did warn you not to meddle in the affairs of important people. After all, look what happened to the hungry fox."

"I don't care about the hungry fox," grumbled Dimnah, "but I suppose you'll go ahead and tell me, anyway."

در اول بکاری که بینت کنیم نظر در صلاح رعیت کنیم
کاود عاوثناکنت وکم خدمت بطوع ورعنت
درمیان بست شیر اوراینهرتبه تقرب ارزانی

The FOX and the RAMS

Two huge rams were fighting one day, clashing their long, curved horns. They fought so hard that they wounded each other, and blood dripped from their heads onto the ground.

A hungry fox tried to creep between them so that he could lick up the blood, but the rams rushed in to attack each other again. The fox was caught between them, and in the fury of their charge he was crushed to death.

"My rage and jealousy are crushing *me* to death!" snarled Dimnah. "I can't bear to see the King whispering and laughing all the time with that stupid bull. *I* was the King's best friend! He used to talk all day long to *me*! I hate Shanzabeh, and I'm going to destroy him."

"And how are you going to do that?" asked Kalilah. "He's a bull. You're a jackal. He's much bigger and stronger than you. And to be frank, dear brother, everyone likes him better than you."

"You don't have to be strong or popular to win," objected Dimnah. "You just have to be cunning, like the jackal who outwitted the snake."

"I like stories about jackals," said Kalilah. "Go on."

The CROW, *the* JACKAL, *and the* SNAKE

A crow once made her nest in a hole in a rocky cliff, but every time she laid a clutch of eggs in it, a poisonous snake, who lived nearby, slithered in and ate them.

One day, as the poor crow wept for the loss of her babies, her friend the jackal came by.

"What's the matter, dear crow?" asked the jackal.

"That evil snake has eaten all my eggs again!" sobbed the crow. "I'm going to get my revenge on him! I'm going to wait until he's asleep and then I'm going to peck his eyes out."

"I wouldn't do that if I were you," advised the jackal. "He strikes like lightning, and one bite would kill you. Look what happened to the heron when he tried to destroy the crab."

"What happened to the heron?" asked the crow.

The CRAB and the HERON

There was once a heron whose home was on the edge of a lake. He lived off the fish he managed to catch, but as he grew older, the fish became too quick for him, and soon he was weak with hunger.

I've lost my quickness and strength, he thought, *so now I must manage through cunning and treachery. Aha! Here comes the crab. Now I'll try my luck.*

And he began to sigh and moan loudly.

"You seem very unhappy, heron," said the crab. "Has something happened to upset you?"

"Oh, yes," wailed the heron. "Such a calamity! I overheard two fishermen talking this morning. They're planning to come here soon and catch every single fish in this lake!"

"That's terrible!" said the crab. "I must warn the fish at once," and off he scuttled.

The fishes' silvery fins quivered with horror when they heard this news.

"There's nothing for it," they said at last. "We'll have to ask our old enemy the heron to help us. Who else is there, after all?"

They swam in a shoal to talk to the heron, who listened to them, his head to one side.

"As it happens," he said at last, "I know of a very good pool near here. Lovely clean water. Wonderfully deep. No fisherman has ever been near it."

"Take us there!" clamoured the fish. "We trust you!"

"Very well," said the heron. "I'll carry you in my beak one by one."

So the fish offered themselves willingly to the heron, who flew them one at a time to the top of a nearby hill and ate them.

After a while the crab became curious about the lovely pool and begged the heron to take him, too.

I'm tired of this busybody crab, thought the heron. *I might as well deal with him, as well.*

So he let the crab fasten his claws around his neck, and off he flew.

When they were up in the sky, the crab saw the bones of all his fishy friends and realized what the heron had been doing. He tightened his grip on the heron's neck — tighter, tighter, tighter! — until the heron plunged lifeless to the ground. The crab, unhurt, hurried back to the lake to tell the fish how they had been duped.

When the jackal finished telling this story, the crow asked, "What has all this got to do with me and the snake?"

"I just wanted to show you that risky plans can go wrong," said the jackal.

"But you haven't told me how to defeat the snake," said the bewildered crow.

"That's easy," said the jackal. "Flutter over people's houses until you see a woman who has set her jewellery out on her roof. Snatch up some pretty piece and fly away with it. The woman will start to shout and scream and will send her people to follow you. Go slowly, making sure they can see you, then drop the jewels on top of the snake. People are scared of snakes. They'll kill it before they dare to pick up their jewellery."

"That's brilliant!" said the crow, and off she flew.

A while later she soared back to the jackal in triumph.

"Your plan worked!" she cried. "The snake is dead, and now I'm going to lay some new eggs and raise my chicks in peace."

"Wait a minute," said Kalila. "I'm confused. Why did you tell me this story?"

Dimnah smiled. "Don't you see? It just shows that if you're cunning you can defeat your enemies. The crow destroyed the snake, and believe me, I'm going to destroy Shanzabeh."

"Be careful, brother," warned Kalilah. "Don't misjudge the bull. He's not only strong but wise and clever, too. Haven't you heard about the hare who tried to trick the fox?"

"You know I haven't," said Dimnah irritably. "Go on."

The HARE, *the* WOLF, *and the* FOX

A hungry wolf was trotting through the forest looking for something to eat when he came upon a hare. The hare started up, paralyzed with such terror that she couldn't run away. But just when she thought she was lost, her wits saved her.

"Oh, noble wolf, I'm much too small to make a meal for you," she said. "But near here lives a fox. He's young and fat, and his flesh must be as tender as can be. Would you like me to show you where he lives?"

The wolf's mouth was watering by now. "I suppose so," he growled through dripping jaws. "Don't try any tricks on me, though."

In fact, a fox really did live nearby, and he had tormented the hare for a long time. As she hopped to his den, the hare laughed to herself at the prospect of getting her revenge.

"Oh, fox, I admire you so much!" said the hare, stepping into the fox's den.

> *"The fame has reached to the ends of the earth*
> *Of your lordly family and noble birth,*
> *Your bushy tail, your sparkling eyes,*
> *Your whiskers so white, and your words so wise!*

"You're so famous, in fact," she went on, "that a holy man has come from far away just to meet you."

"A holy man, eh?" said the fox. "He's a welcome guest, of course. Why don't you bring him here into my den?"

The hare bounded outside, delighted with her success, but the fox was no fool, and the hare's flattery hadn't deceived him for a moment.

That hare's a tricky one, he thought. *It's a good thing I'm prepared for something like this to happen.*

At the back of his den the fox had earlier dug a pit and covered it with sticks and straw, just in case he was ever visited by an enemy. So when the hare led the wolf, who was desperate for his dinner, into the fox's den, they both fell through the thin layer of sticks into the deep, dark pit while the fox ran away to safety.

"You've cheated me!" snarled the wolf, and he fell upon the hare and killed her.

"There you are, you see," said Kalilah. "Treachery is of no use against a strong and cunning enemy. You'd better not try anything on Shanzabeh."

"Huh!" snorted Dimnah. "That stupid bull is all puffed up with pride and, anyway, he has no idea how much I hate him. He won't be on his guard. I'll tell you about another hare who got the better of a lion, though he was so little and weak."

The HARE and the LION

In another land not far away there was a beautiful meadow full of perfumed flowers through which ran a stream of crystal-clear water. It was home to many animals living in harmony with one another. But their lives were made miserable by a lion, who preyed on them and filled them with terror.

At last the animals went to the lion to make a bargain. If, they said, he stopped hunting them, they would send him one animal every day to satisfy his hunger so that the others could live in peace.

The lion agreed, and so it went on until it was the turn of the hare to be sacrificed.

"Trust me," she said to her friends. "I'll put an end to this."

She waited until a whole hour had passed after the lion's usual breakfast time and he was furious with hunger. Then she meekly approached him.

"Sir," she said, "I'm so small that I'm supposed to make up only half of your breakfast. But the other hare who was to come with me was seized by another lion. It leaped out on us as we were coming along here to you, and I only just managed to escape. I tried to explain that we belonged to you, but he started to insult you and said that *he* was the lord here now."

The lion was enraged. "Another lion?" he roared. "He says he's the lord here, does he? Take me to him, hare."

The hare led the lion to a deep well in which the water was so still that everything above was perfectly reflected in it.

"Oh, oh!" cried the hare. "I'm so frightened! Protect me, lion!" And she jumped into the lion's arms.

The lion, peering into the well, saw another lion with a hare in his grip.
With a terrifying snarl he threw the real hare to the ground, leaped into the
well, and was drowned.

"So there you are, Kalilah," Dimnah said triumphantly. "If a hare can outwit a lion, I can certainly outwit that stupid bull. I'm not listening to another word from you."

And off he went to court.

As Dimnah approached the King, he let his tail droop and his ears flop and he hung his head so that he was the picture of misery.

"Dimnah!" said the King. "You seem very miserable. Has something happened?"

Dimnah heaved a great sigh. "Yes, my lord, but I hardly dare speak of it."

The King took him aside so that no one else could hear. "What is it? Tell me at once," he commanded.

Slowly, with many hesitations, Dimnah said, "It has come to my ears, O King, that Shanzabeh the bull has been plotting with your army and courtiers. 'The lion is weak,' he's been telling them. 'He's not worthy to be our ruler.'"

"Are you sure of this?" the King asked with a troubled frown.

"I am, sire. Your Majesty has shown such favour to this treacherous bull that he's swollen with pride. He thinks he deserves to be king in your place. Things have gone so far that you must deal with him quickly if you're to save your kingdom."

The King was distressed to hear that his friend wanted to destroy him, and at first he could not believe it. "How could my dear Shanzabeh treat me in this way," he asked, "when I have been so kind to him?"

"Easily," said Dimnah with a sorrowful shake of the head. "Remember how the scorpion turned on the tortoise."

The SCORPION and the TORTOISE

A scorpion and a tortoise were once close friends, living together happily. One day they set out on a journey. Before long they came to a river. The scorpion looked anxiously at the water, then said, "My friend, I can't swim. You'll have to cross the river alone and go on without me."

"I wouldn't leave you behind for the world," said the tortoise. "Climb on my back and I'll carry you over."

So the scorpion scrambled onto the tortoise's back, and the tortoise began to swim across the river.

After a while the tortoise felt a tapping on his back. "What are you doing, scorpion?"

"Oh, I'm trying out my sting against your shell."

"What? But I'm your friend! I'm even taking you across the river!"

"I can't help that," said the scorpion. "It's my nature to sting whoever I can, whether it's a friend or an enemy."

"So you see," Dimnah said, "it's the nature of a traitor to betray. Shanzabeh simply can't help himself."

The King agreed at last that Shanzabeh might be his enemy, but he was still not afraid of him. "He eats only grass while I kill and eat other animals," he said. "It is he who should be afraid of me, not I of him."

"But your soldiers, my lord! Your nobles, whom Shanzabeh has turned against you!" said Dimnah cunningly. "Think of the harm they can do to you!"

"What should I do then?"

"Kill him. You must kill Shanzabeh, and without delay," Dinmah said boldly, hatred rising in his throat.

"No, no," said the King. "I'll talk to him and judge the matter for myself." This worried Dimnah.

Shanzabeh is sure to talk the King round, he thought, *and my plotting will be exposed.*

Aloud he said, "That would be dangerous, sire. Shanzabeh is ready to act against you and will strike first. Let me go and talk to him. I'll try to find out exactly what he's planning, then I'll return and report to you."

He left the King's presence, smiling with glee at his own cleverness, but as he approached Shanzabeh, he put on the same dejected look with which he had earlier approached the King.

Shanzabeh greeted him kindly. "Are you well, Dimnah? You look unhappy today."

"Dear Shanzabeh, I'm the bearer of bad news," replied Dimnah sadly. "You know how fickle kings can be, showing favour one moment and violent hostility the next."

"What are you trying to tell me?" asked Shanzabeh anxiously. "Has the King turned against you?"

"Not against me, dear friend. Against you! I heard him say with my own ears, 'Shanzabeh has become wonderfully fat with all the favour I've shown him. How delicious his flesh must be! It's time that I and my beasts should feast upon him.' You must believe me, Shanzabeh. You know what a true friend I've always been to you. I've come here to warn you."

Shanzabeh stared at him, astonished and distressed. "I can't believe this! The King has always been so kind to me, and I have served him loyally. Those worthless courtiers of his must have told him false tales, and when a lie comes in through the door, the truth flies out through the window. The King is being deceived, like the poor goose who saw the moon."

"I haven't heard that story," said Dimnah. "Tell it to me."

The GOOSE and the MOON

A poor goose saw the reflection of the moon in a pool of water. He thought it was a fish and tried to catch it. He tried again and again without success, of course.

He became so discouraged that the next time he saw a real fish in the pool he did not even try to catch it, thinking it was only a reflection of the moon. The goose gave up eating altogether and sadly starved to death.

همان حاصل تشنه است از مشاهدهٔ سراب

"Oh, the poor thing," murmured Dimnah with false sympathy.

"But I still can't understand it," said Shanzabeh. "Why has the King turned against me? I've done nothing wrong. I've always been loyal and have treated him with great respect. Could it be, I wonder, that his pride has made him hate me? Or has he been turned against me by jealous flatterers?"

Dimnah said nothing.

Shanzabeh sighed. "I should have known better than to trust a lion. I've heard it said that it's safer to swim with a crocodile than to be close to a king. Just think of the hawk who argued with a chicken!"

"I don't know that story," Dimnah said, pretending to be interested. "Why don't you tell it to me?"

The HAWK *and the* CHICKEN

A hawk and a chicken were talking one day.

"You're very ungrateful," the hawk said to the chicken.

"What makes you say that?" asked the chicken.

"Why, men feed you and give you water and a house to live in and protect you from all kinds of danger, and yet whenever they come near you, you run away and try to hide. I, on the other hand, am a wild thing, hunting my own food, and yet if they offer me only a morsel or two from their hands, I give them all the prey I catch as soon as I hear them call."

"You come to men's calls because you've never seen a hawk roasting on a spit," retorted the chicken. "But I've seen too many of my brothers and sisters cooking in a frying pan."

"The reason I've told you this story, Dimnah," Shanzabeh said sadly, shaking his massive head, "is to explain how I forgot, being so happy in the King's friendship, that I might be in danger like the poor chicken."

نظم مرغ دست آموز را چندانکه کس دور افکند   با نشاط مال آید باز چون کوـ
ماکیان جواب داد که راست میگویی

Dimnah nodded, pretending to be serious and sad. "What do you intend
to do now, dear Shanzabeh?"

Shanzabeh sighed. "What can I do? If my fate is to die, I'll die. I can't
escape my destiny. I shall take my lead from the nightingale."

"Why?" asked Dimnah. "What did the nightingale do?"

"I'll tell you the story," said Shanzabeh.

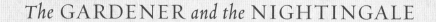

There was once a gardener whose garden was his joy and delight. Many lovely flowers bloomed there, but one bush bore roses that were so fragrant and beautiful that the gardener loved them more than anything else in the world.

A nightingale lived in the garden, and every night she sang her sweet song to the moon. She, too, loved the roses, and rubbed her face against them until the petals fell to the ground.

The gardener was incensed when he saw his precious roses being destroyed by the nightingale.

He set a trap beside the rose bush and caught her. Then he locked her in a cage.

"You took my darling roses away from me," he cried, "and I'm taking your freedom away from you."

"That's hardly fair," objected the nightingale. "Surely, I don't deserve to be imprisoned because I accidentally destroyed a few roses? Don't you know that if you're unjust to someone you'll regret it later and be punished in your turn?"

The gardener saw the justice of this. His anger had cooled by now, so he released the nightingale, who was filled with gratitude.

"You've been kind to me and now I'll reward you," said the nightingale. "If you dig under your rose bush, you'll find a pot full of treasure."

The gardener did as she suggested, and out of the ground came a hoard of gold just as the nightingale had promised. The gardener was overjoyed, but something puzzled him.

"Nightingale," he asked, "how is it that you saw a pot of gold under the earth when you didn't see the snare I set for you above it?"

"Ah," said the nightingale, "it was my destiny to fall into your hands and there was nothing I could do to prevent it."

When Shanzabeh finished telling his story, Dimnah did not know what to say. It sounded as if the bull had accepted his fate already.

At last he said, "It's not because of you, or because of anyone else, that you've fallen out of favour. The fault is all with the King. He's like a snake whose skin is smooth and brilliantly coloured on the outside, but whose fangs contain a deadly poison."

"I should never have tried to be close to him," moaned Shanzabeh. "How foolish I've been! I should have known that a lion will always seek to kill and eat one of my kind. Oh, my poor head is swimming! I feel as if I've been sucked into a whirlwind of destruction. I was blinded by greed and ambition. I ought to have stayed in my own lush meadow where I was happy all day long."

"You're right, I suppose," agreed Dimnah. "Greed is at the root of every trouble. Do you know the story of the hunter who tried to catch the fox?"

"No," replied Shanzabeh. "Tell it to me."

The HUNTER and the FOX

A hunter was travelling about one day, looking for something to catch, when he saw a fox whose tail was bushy and sleek and a fine bright red. *That tail would fetch a tidy bit of money*, thought the hunter, so he dug a pit near the fox's den and covered it with sticks to disguise it. Then he put a big piece of meat beside the sticks as bait, hoping the fox would try to eat the meat and fall into his trap. Finally, he hid behind a rock and waited.

But the fox was too clever for the hunter.

"Hmm, what's that?" the fox asked, peering at the meat from a distance. "It looks like a tasty meal, but there's something not quite right about it. And I don't like those sticks. I'll go and hunt for my dinner somewhere else."

And off he trotted.

Nearby, though, was a greedy leopard. When he saw the tempting piece of meat, he pounced on it and fell into the pit.

The hunter, behind his rock, heard the crash and was sure he had caught the fox. Without thinking, he ran up to the pit and jumped in, too, eager to kill the fox and cut off his tail.

A man and a leopard in a pit? You can guess what happened next!

Oh, Shanzabeh, you were a fool indeed
To trust the friendship of a fickle King.
He's like the hunter blinded by his greed.
You are his prey, and he will crouch, and spring.

"What can I do, dear Dimnah?" asked Shanzabeh. "The King's friends are plotting against me, I know. I'll end up like the poor camel — and you know what happened to him."

"No, I don't," said Dimnah. "Tell me."

وابن مثل بدان آوردم تابدابى كه

The CAMEL *and the* LION

here was once a lion whose humble servants were a crow, a wolf, and a jackal. A stray camel wandered across their path. He saw at once that he could not protect himself from such fierce animals, so he decided to throw himself on their mercy and offer to serve them. The lion accepted him as a member of their group, and for a while all went well.

But one day, when the lion was out hunting, he was attacked by a furious elephant and was badly wounded. He crept back to his lair and lay there helpless.

"What are we going to do now?" the crow, the jackal, and the wolf asked one another. "The lion always catches our food for us. We live off the scraps he leaves behind. But now he's too weak to hunt anything."

All their eyes turned to the camel.

"There's our answer," whispered the wolf. "The camel's meat will feed us all until the lion is well again."

"Yes," said the jackal, "but the lion won't agree to kill him. He promised the camel his protection. He'd never break his word."

"I've thought of a plan," said the crow. "We must all go to the lion and one by one offer to sacrifice ourselves to be eaten by the others. The three of us will object to eating one another for various reasons, but we'll all agree, sadly, to eat the camel."

So off they went to visit the sick lion, with the camel trailing after them.

"Oh, dear lion," the crow began, "I can't bear to see you so weak and hungry. Look, my life is worthless without you. I'm offering my own body as food for you all to share."

The jackal shook his head. "It's very good of you, crow, but what use would that be? You're much too small to make a meal for the rest of us. No, I'll volunteer to die. You can eat me."

"You!" scoffed the wolf. "The flesh of a jackal is horrible to eat, as everyone knows. It would be better to sacrifice me."

"We couldn't do that!" cried the crow and the jackal together. "Your meat would be even worse than the jackal's. It would poison us."

"Well," said the camel bravely, "I can see where this is going. You've been my friends up till now. You've protected me all this time, and now I'll pay my debt. Kill me and eat my flesh."

"Oh, how very good you are, dear camel!" cried the others, and without a moment's hesitation they fell on him, eager to begin their dinner.

"I want to be like that camel, you see," said Shanzabeh. "He died with dignity and honour, and I'm determined to do the same."

"Oh, it may not come to that," said Dimnah. "Perhaps you should try to talk the lion round again. Otherwise you'll end up like the Spirit of the Ocean, who was cruel to the sandpipers."

"Why? What did he do?" asked Shanzabeh.

"I'll tell you," said Dimnah.

The SPIRIT of the OCEAN and the SANDPIPERS

A pair of sandpipers who lived on the shores of the Indian Ocean wanted to build a nest where the hen could lay her eggs.

"Why don't you lay them right here?" asked her husband. "This is a good enough place to raise a family. It's quite delightful, in fact, and besides, where else would we go?"

"Oh, I don't know," replied the hen sandpiper. "I'm worried that we're too close to the sea. The tide might come in and wash our little ones away."

"The tide?" scoffed her husband. "It won't get the better of *me*. I'll demand justice from heaven if the sea harms us. I'll have my revenge on him."

"That's ridiculous!" said his wife. "How can you, a little bird, get the better of the mighty ocean? You're as silly as the tortoise, and if you're not careful, you'll come to a bad end like he did."

"Why? What happened to him?"

"I thought you knew this story," said his wife, "but you obviously don't, so here it is."

The TORTOISE and the GEESE

A talkative tortoise once lived beside a pond with a pair of geese, who were his friends. But one hot summer the pond dried up completely so that there were no fish for the geese to catch and no water for the tortoise to drink.

"We'll have to fly off and find another pond," the geese told the tortoise.

"Oh, my dear friends, don't leave me here alone!" cried the tortoise. "I'll die of misery without you! Just think of all the good times we've shared!" And he began to tell story after story, reminding his friends of all the things they had done.

The geese thought for a while and came up with a plan. They decided to hold a stick between them in their beaks. The tortoise could hang on to the middle of it with his mouth and be carried through the air.

"But you must promise faithfully not to open your mouth to speak," said the geese solemnly to the tortoise. "No talking at all or you'll fall to your death."

"I can be quiet when I have to be," the tortoise said, offended. "I'll keep my mouth clamped tight around that stick, I assure you."

So the geese flew into the air with the tortoise between them, hanging on to the stick.

Soon they passed over a village, and all the people came out to see such an extraordinary sight.

"Ha-ha! Look at that!" one shouted.

"Whoever saw anything so ridiculous!" cried another

"That's the funniest thing I've seen in my whole life!" said a third.

At last the tortoise could bear their mockery no longer and shouted, "I hope God blinds you, you rude, silly people!"

But, of course, as soon as he opened his mouth, he let go of the stick and fell.

"And I'm telling you this, Shanzabeh," Dimnah said, "because you should listen to me and take my advice, unlike the tortoise, who didn't listen to the geese."

"Yes, but what happened to the sandpipers and their eggs?" asked tender-hearted Shanzabeh.

"Oh, yes," said Dimnah, "I forgot about them. Well, the hen did lay her eggs on the shore, and a great wave did come up out of the sea and carried them away. Her husband was furious and reported the sea to all the other birds, who went in a huge fluttering crowd to ask the phoenix for help. The phoenix called his army of helpers. It was a great army, too, with feathery armour and coats of mail. Their weapons were their stabbing beaks and slashing claws. The phoenix, his army, and all the birds swooped down on the sea, and the Spirit of the Ocean was so frightened that he sent another wave to roll the sandpipers' eggs out of the water and back into their nest."

"Why did you tell me this story?" asked Shanzabeh, puzzled.

"To show you that you have to be careful when you're dealing with a powerful enemy," said Dimnah patiently. "The sandpiper could do nothing by himself. He needed the phoenix and all his troops to help him. Who's going to help you if you confront the King of Lions on your own? You don't have the army of the phoenix to support you like the sandpiper did."

"Well, anyway," said Shanzabeh, "whatever you say, I'm still going to see the King. I can't believe he's really turned against me."

Dimnah was worried now.

What will happen to me if this crafty bull wheedles his way back into the King's favour? he thought. *My plotting will be discovered and the King will take his revenge.*

He went to talk to Kalilah.

"How are things going with all your foolish plans?" his brother asked him.

"I've almost succeeded in getting rid of Shanzabeh," Dimnah answered, trying to sound sure of himself. "That stupid bull is on his way to see the King now. We'll go with him, and you'll see how it will end."

So Shanzabeh, accompanied by Kalilah and Dimnah, trotted off to see the King.

As soon as the King caught sight of Shanzabeh, the lies Dimnah had told worked like poison through his body. He roared and lashed his tail and ground his sharp white teeth.

Shanzabeh saw that he was in deadly peril. *I'll have to fight for my life,* he told himself.

The King of Lions launched himself onto the bull's back, but Shanzabeh fought with desperate courage. Terrible sounds filled the air — the bellows of the bull, the roars of the King, and the clash of boulders under their feet — as the former friends rolled about, locked in deadly combat. All the wild animals far and near fled in terror into the mountains.

At last the King won the battle, and Shanzabeh's poor bloodied body lay dead at his feet.

> *The noble bull lies vanquished in the dust,*
> *Brought by a trick to a sorry end.*
> *Dimnah the jackal has betrayed his trust,*
> *And the King has lost his dearest friend.*

Dimnah had watched the battle between the lion and bull with undisguised delight, but Kalilah shook his head.

"This is wrong, Dimnah. You've done a terrible thing and you shouldn't take pleasure in the death of poor Shanzabeh. I've tried again and again to warn you, but you refused to listen to me. You must be especially careful now."

"Careful? Why should I be careful?" retorted Dimnah, washing his whiskers unconcernedly. "I've got what I wanted. I destroyed my enemy, and the King is sure to make me his closest friend again."

"I doubt it," said Kalilah. "Anyway, I'm tired of talking to you. You disgust me. And I'm afraid that if I try to help you, I'll end up like the bird in the story."

"What bird? What story?" asked Dimnah, who was only half listening.

زغوغای ایشان وحوش وسباع

وکار من با نوهمین مزاج دارد و مزاوقانت

The BIRD and the MONKEYS

Once there was a troop of monkeys who lived in a tree. They were happy enough in the summer, but then winter came. Soon the frost made the ground as hard as stone, icicles hung from every twig, and the wind was so bitterly cold that the monkeys were in danger of freezing to death.

"If only we could light a fire to warm ourselves!" they moaned one night as they shivered on a bare branch.

Just then one of them spotted a firefly dancing in the darkness.

"Fire! A spark of fire!" cried the monkeys.

They leaped down from the tree, caught the firefly, and piled twigs and sticks onto it, then bent and blew until their cheeks nearly burst, trying to make their precious spark flare into a blaze.

A bird flying past saw what they were doing. "That firefly won't help you," he called to them. "It's an insect with a shiny tail, not a spark of fire."

The monkeys took no notice. The bird watched for a while, trying to tell them their efforts were hopeless, but they refused to listen. At last he flew down and landed among them.

"Didn't you hear what I've been trying to tell you?" he asked. "A firefly —"

But the monkeys, enraged with the bird, turned on him and tore off his head.

"That story describes how I feel, Dimnah," said Kalilah. "I'm like the bird who's been wasting my breath, and if I spend more time trying to give advice to a villain like you, I'll end up in as much trouble as the bird."

Dimnah was shocked to hear that his brother had turned against him.

"Oh, please, please, dear Kalilah," he said, "don't stop giving me advice. I do listen to you. Really I do."

"Well, listen to this then," said Kalilah sternly. "It's a story about a swindler and a fool."

The SWINDLER and the FOOL

The swindler, whose name was Sharp-Wit, and the fool, who was called Light-Heart, were travelling along a road one day when they found a bag of gold on the ground.

"What luck!" said Sharp-Wit. "A chance like this doesn't come along very often."

"Let's divide it up now," said Light-Heart, "then, when we get to the town, we can each spend our share as we like."

But Sharp-Wit saw how he could swindle Light-Heart. "No," he said, "it would be better to take just enough to pay our way for the next few days. We can bury the rest under this tree and come back for more when we need it. We're less likely to lose it if it's safely stored here."

Foolish Light-Heart agreed, and off the two of them went to the town. As soon as he could, Sharp-Wit the swindler hurried back to the tree and dug up the gold, while Light-Heart was still enjoying himself in the town.

When Light-Heart began to run out of money, he went to Sharp-Wit and suggested they should go back to the tree to retrieve the rest of the gold.

"Certainly," said Sharp-Wit heartily.

They got to the tree and dug, but of course the gold wasn't there.

"You thief!" cried Sharp-Wit, who had planned all this in advance. He caught Light-Heart by the collar and shouted, "You came back and stole all the gold! I'm going to take you to the judge and make you give it back!"

Poor Light-Heart did his best to deny Sharp-Wit's lies, but Sharp-Wit dragged him in front of the judge.

"How can you prove this man stole all the gold?" the judge asked Sharp-Wit.

"The tree alone is my witness," said Sharp-Wit, "and I shall pray that it will speak for me."

"What nonsense is this?" scoffed the judge. "A tree can't speak!"

"If Your Excellency will come and see for yourself," said Sharp-Wit, "I'm sure my prayer will be heard and the tree will speak up for me."

Sharp-Wit hurried home and said to his father, "Please help me. The tree where I buried the gold is hollow. Hide in it tonight and speak out for me tomorrow. The judge will think the tree is speaking."

His father was shocked at Sharp-Wit's wickedness. "My boy," he said, "swindling is a risky business. Be careful you don't end up like the frog."

"Why?" asked Sharp-Wit. "What happened to the frog?"

The FROG, the CRAB, the SNAKE, and the WEASEL

There was once a frog whose life was made miserable by a snake, who came to her pool and ate up her children one by one. At last the frog complained to a crab.

"You must lay a trap for the snake," said the crab. "Catch some fish and place them in a line between the den of the snake and the lair of the weasel. The weasel will follow the line of fish, and when he's eaten them all up, he'll attack the snake and eat him, too."

The frog thought that this was an excellent idea and did as the crab suggested. When all the fish were gone, the frog thought her plan had worked, but though the weasel had enjoyed the fish, he did not want to risk attacking the snake.

The next day, when he was hungry again, the weasel went to see if any more fish had appeared. But when he came to the pool, he caught sight of the frog and ate her and the rest of her children until all of them were gone.

"And the moral of the story is this," the old man said, shaking his finger at his son, "deceit is dangerous and the deceiver always comes to a bad end."

"Oh, please, Father, help me just this once," begged Sharp-Wit. "I promise it's the last time I'll swindle anyone."

He went on and on in the same way until at last his father agreed.

The next morning the old man hid in the hollow tree and waited until Sharp-Wit, Light-Heart, and the judge appeared.

"Well, tree?" asked the judge, feeling a little silly at talking to a tree, "did you see who took the gold?"

"Oo-oo, yes!" hooted Sharp-Wit's father in a spooky voice. "It was that wicked Light-Heart who did it!"

The judge was no fool, however. "Light a fire under this tree," he told his servants.

So they lit a fire under the tree, and Sharp-Wit's father burst out of it, choking from the smoke and half burned up.

"I confess!" he croaked. "It was all the fault of my son, Sharp-Wit. He made me help him swindle you!"

Then he fell down and died. The judge condemned Sharp-Wit heartily, while Light-Heart recovered his money and went away a happy man.

"That's the sort of thing that can happen when you deceive people," Kalilah said severely when the story was ended. "As Sharp-Wit's father told him, the deceiver never wins out in the end."

"I'm not scared of anything," said Dimnah boldly. "I've been very clever, and nothing bad will happen to me. I may be two-faced, but what of it? A rose has two sides, but it's the most beautiful flower in the garden. A nib is split up the middle, but it writes valuable words."

Kalilah said angrily,

"You're not a rose! You're a spiteful thorn.
You leave your enemies bleeding and torn.
The nib of a pen? You're more like a snake,
And your forked tongue leaves death in its wake.

"I'll never forgive you for what you've done to Shanzabeh, Dimnah, and I don't want to have anything more to do with you. If I do, I'll end up like the gardener."

"What gardener?" asked Dimnah, who was beginning to feel worried at the thought of losing his friend and brother.

The GARDENER and the BEAR

There was once a gardener whose estate was as lovely as the Garden of Eden. The leaves of the trees spread and shimmered like the tails of peacocks, and each rose was as beautiful as an emperor's crown. Apples shone like lamps among the branches of the apple trees, quinces glowed as yellow as the sun, oranges nestled like golden balls among the bright green leaves, and the scent of lemons perfumed the air. The pomegranate seeds were as red as rubies and the figs were like candies.

The gardener loved his garden so much that he spent all his days and all his nights alone there with only his plants for company. He never returned home and quite forgot his family and friends who, in their turn, forgot about him.

At last, however, he began to feel lonely. *Oranges and lemons are all very well,* he told himself, *but they're not the same as friends. A friend! That's what I need. A friend.*

So he pushed open the garden gate and went outside into the wide, open plain, looking for someone to talk to.

By chance a bear was also feeling lonely that day. He had wandered down from the hilltops and was searching for company, too. He was an ugly old thing, with shaggy fur and a shambling way of walking, but he was the first creature that the gardener had seen for a long time. His heart leaped for joy at the sight of this kindly looking animal, so he opened the gate of his garden again and invited the bear to come in.

Soon the two of them were devoted companions. They wandered happily around the garden and enjoyed the delicious fruits. In the hot afternoons, when the gardener was sleepy, he would lie under a tree and the bear would fan his face to drive off flies.

One day, however, there were so many flies, and they pestered the gardener so persistently, that the bear decided to deal with them once and for all. He picked up a huge stone, wanting to crush them, and brought it down on the gardener's head. Of course, the flies flitted out of the way, but the gardener never drew another breath.

"That's a stupid story," retorted Dimnah. "I'm not a fool like that bear. I would never harm you."

"I'm not so sure," said Kalilah. "Your selfishness has blinded you and made you treacherous. I've told you, Dimnah. Stay away from me from now on. I'm not your friend any longer."

And so the two of them went on, arguing about what Dimnah had done.

In the meantime the King of Lions had begun to feel sorry for killing his friend the bull.

Shanzabeh was so good and so wise. I shall miss his friendship sorely, he thought. *Was he really my enemy? Or have I been deceived? Perhaps I was too hasty. I had only Dimnah's word to go on, after all.*

He confided his sorrow and regret to a leopard, who shook his head and said, "What's done is done, Your Majesty. Nothing will bring your friend Shanzabeh back to you now. Don't hanker after the impossible, or you may lose what you have, as the fox in the story did."

"The fox?" said the lion. "Why, what happened?"

here was onc   n from which most
of the meat h   f a meal, but it was
better than no

The fox pic   ing it home when
he saw some fat ch   e fox dropped the
skin and began to   hickens instead.

At that moment   , fox," he said.

"I *am* puzzled," s   ow to steal one of
those chickens."

"Forget them," s   ose chickens for a
long time, but the n   nd watchful that I
never get near them.   Isn't that enough
for you?"

"This little scrap?   a mouthful. And,
anyway, what's a pie   en?"

"You should be ha   fox. "Otherwise
you'll lose it, just like

"What happened t   the fox.

"I'll tell you," said t

The DONKEY'S TAIL

nce there was a poor donkey who had no tail. He went searching everywhere, hoping to find one, and at last he came to a field full of ripe, golden corn.

"I'm sure my tail must be in the middle of that field," the donkey said to himself, so he ran into the field and rampaged about in the ripe corn hunting for his tail. The farmer, furious to see his crop being trampled, caught hold of the donkey and cut off both his ears to teach him a lesson.

"The point is," the jackal said at last, "that if the donkey hadn't gone looking for his tail, he wouldn't have lost his ears."

"I don't care about your donkeys and your farmers," said the fox. "I'm going to catch myself a chicken." And he darted into the middle of the flock and tried to fasten his teeth on a plump little bird.

The chicken keeper saw him at once and chased him away. At the very same moment a bird, flying high in the sky, spotted the piece of skin, swooped down, and carried it away.

The King scratched his puzzled head with a huge paw when the story was over. "I don't quite see . . ." he began.

"Well, sire," the leopard explained, "the point of the story is that the fox never had a chicken for his supper and he even lost his piece of skin. You've lost Shanzabeh. You can't bring him back, but if you spend all your time thinking about him and feeling sorry for yourself, you'll neglect your courtiers, your servants, and your soldiers, and you'll lose all of them, too."

The King of Lions listened thoughtfully to the leopard's wise words and decided to find out once and for all whether Shanzabeh had been plotting to overthrow him or not.

"For if he was a traitor," the King said, "I shall be able to put him out of my mind and be a proper monarch again." Then he asked the leopard to investigate and find out what he could.

The leopard was an expert at hiding in secret places. He could lurk in quiet corners without being seen. He slipped about silently, using his eyes and his ears, and happened by chance to be passing the den of Kalilah and Dimnah when Kalilah was once again scolding Dimnah for betraying the bull.

"I know I was wrong to betray Shanzabeh," Dimnah was saying, "but the temptation was so great! Can't you forgive me, dear Kalilah?"

Aha! thought the leopard. *Here's the truth of the matter. I never trusted that cunning jackal from the start. But what should I do now? The King is fond of Dimnah. If I tell him the truth, he may not believe me and may turn against me just as he turned on Shanzabeh. This secret might lead to more trouble for everyone.*

Then he remembered the King's mother.

I'll go to her, he decided. *I must tell someone, after all. But I'll ask her to keep it a secret in case all of this trouble lands back on my poor head.*

So off he went.

The next day the King's mother visited her son as she did every day. "Why do you look so sad?" she asked him.

"Oh, Mother! I can't forget poor Shanzabeh," said the King. "I miss him every minute of the day. The advice he gave me was always so good. How can I continue to reign without him? If only I knew if he had really betrayed me or not."

His mother hesitated. "I have heard something about this," she said, "but I promised to keep it a secret."

"Tell me, Mother, please," begged the King.

He pleaded so hard that at last she said, "The leopard told me that the culprit is the jackal Dimnah. He lied to you, my son. Shanzabeh was innocent."

"Dimnah!" cried the King. "I knew it!"

The King summoned all his courtiers, ministers, chiefs, and nobles, and told them to bring Dimnah in front of his royal throne.

Dimnah trotted confidently up to the throne, but when he saw that the King would not look at him and had turned his face away, he began to be very afraid.

"Why does the King look so thoughtful?" he asked a servant standing nearby.

The King's mother overheard him and burst out angrily, "His Majesty is deciding whether you should live or die. He knows what a traitor you are."

Dimnah thought quickly and said, "I should have known this would happen if I offered my friendly advice to the King. Jealous enemies have been spreading stories about me. I've always been sincere and have devoted myself to His Majesty. If I'd been guilty, would I have come here of my own accord? I would have gone away and spared myself all this trouble."

And he went on and on, protesting his innocence with all his usual cleverness, telling marvellous stories until the King and the whole court were confused and uncertain about whether he was guilty or not.

At last a lynx, who was a faithful friend and servant of the King, turned to Dimnah and said, "You have a lot to say about the dangers of serving a king and the envy of others. You should have thought less about yourself and more about your duty and service. I'll tell you a story about a man who was truly loyal despite the treatment he received."

سید اعلی آورد نداز وی اعراض نمود خود را

The SHEIKH and the HOLY MAN

Once there was a great sheikh who was the leader of a community of saintly men. Nearby lived a poor holy man, who spent his time wandering here and there looking for a master to teach him true religion. The holy man heard about this great sheikh, who was so wise and knowledgeable, and he came to visit him. But when he knocked on the sheikh's door, a servant told him to go away.

"The sheikh isn't here," the servant told him. "He's gone to pay his respects to the king."

The holy man was shocked when he heard this, and stumped off angrily to the local town.

"A true saint doesn't bow and scrape to a king," he said out loud, not caring who heard him. "He should think about nothing except prayer and study."

Now, that very morning a thief was being pursued around the town.

"Look at that ragged man mumbling to himself!" someone shouted. "He's the thief! I recognize him!"

"I'm not a thief! I'm innocent!" the holy man cried indignantly, but no one believed him, and he was dragged away to have his hand cut off.

Luckily, when the executioner's knife was about to fall on his hand, the sheikh appeared, riding home on his fine Arabian horse.

"Is this person really a thief?" he asked the officer in charge. "He looks like a holy man to me."

Just then the sheikh's servant came up. "This person visited you this morning, sir," he said to the sheikh. "He's a holy man and wants you to be his teacher."

The holy man was released, but instead of being angry at the treatment he had received, he spent the rest of his life as the sheikh's humble servant, learning from him the true path to the holy life.

"What's the point of your story?" asked Dimnah cheekily when the lynx finished. "I didn't understand a word of it."

"It shows that even great and holy sheikhs aren't above visiting kings and showing respect to them," said the lynx sternly. "So who do you think you are, a poor little jackal, to set yourself up so high and mighty as the King's favourite adviser?"

The King had been thinking while all this was going on. "Dimnah, I'm going to get to the truth of all this," he said. "I'm going to find out exactly what happened."

Dimnah pretended to look pleased. "Oh, yes, Your Majesty! That's just what I want, too. You'll find out how innocent I am. I know you will."

"That may be," said the King, "but in the meantime I'm going to send you off to prison."

When Dimnah was led away in chains, the King's mother saw how her son sat in silence, heavy-hearted. "What's wrong?" she asked him.

"I can't believe Dimnah is guilty of this terrible deed," said the King, shaking his mighty head. "He's such an amusing and clever fellow. I used to enjoy his company all the time before Shanzabeh came along. I can't believe he would be so cruel, plotting Shanzabeh's death in that wicked way."

"It's not hard to understand," his mother said. "You favoured Shanzabeh over him and he became eaten up with envy."

"It's true," said the King, sighing, "that envy is like a fire that burns up everything in its path."

It was night by now, and the King's servants had long since gone to bed. The lion and his mother went off to sleep, and soon only Dimnah was awake. He lay shivering with cold in his prison cell, and the heavy chains that bound him clanked every time he moved.

Someone tapped softly at the cell door.

"Who . . . who's there?" he called out nervously, afraid that the executioner had come for him.

"It's only your brother," said a dear familiar voice, and into the prison crept Kalilah.

Kalilah was shocked to see how miserable Dimnah looked, his ears drooping, his fur bedraggled, his head held low. In spite of himself, he could not help tears falling from his eyes.

"Oh, dear Dimnah!" he cried. "How am I going to live without you? How can I bear to lose my brother?"

"Don't mourn for me, Kalilah," Dimnah said sadly. "I have only myself to blame. You tried many times to teach me what was right, but I wouldn't listen. I knew all the time that what I was doing was wrong, but I was swept away with greed and envy. I don't complain. I deserve to die."

The light of morning was brightening the sky, and Kalilah was afraid of being found in the prison.

"Farewell, my poor brother," he said at last, then stole away past the sleeping guards to find a place where he could cry undisturbed.

That day the King ordered that no more food or drink should be brought to Dimnah in his prison, and so when a few days had passed, he died, full of bitter regret for what he had done to Shanzabeh.

All this time the Shah had been listening intently to the counsellor's stories of the two crafty jackals.

"How clever you are, my dear friend," he said. "Next time someone tries to flatter me or gives me bad advice I'll remember Kalilah and Dimnah. I'll think twice before I act and make sure that all my decisions are just and fair."

"If you do that, sire," said the counsellor, "you'll be a great and noble ruler and your people will remember your name with gratitude forever."

And he smiled his wise smile as he went silently away.

وكفت اى برادر نژاد درين بلاو محنت

ILLUSTRATION CREDITS

All the illustrations reproduced in this book are from the manuscript *Anwar-i Suhayli* (*Lights of Canopus*) housed in the Aga Khan Museum in Toronto, Canada. Here they are shown in full.

Anwar-i Suhayli (*Lights of Canopus*)
Rendered into Persian by
Husayn ibn 'Ali
al-Wa'iz al-Kashifi
Illustrations attributed
to Sadiqi Beg
Qazvin, Iran, 1593
Opaque watercolour,
gold, ink, paper
AKM289

Pages 6 and 7: Front and back binding of *Anwar-i Suhayli*.

Page 11: The King of Lions' court, with Shanzabeh at a distance, folio 44r.

Page 13: The King of Lions' court, with jackals and a leopard, folio 50v.

Page 14: The fox and the drum, folio 52v.

Page 17: Shanzabeh and Dimnah before the King of Lions, folio 55r.

Page 18: The fox crushed by two rams, folio 56r.

Page 19: The jackal addresses the crow, folio 63v.

Page 20: The crab and the heron, folio 64r.

Page 23: The fox and the hare converse, folio 67r.

Page 25: The hare and the lion look into the well, folio 69v.

Page 27: The scorpion rides across the river on the tortoise's back, folio 74r.

Page 28: The goose pecks at the moon's reflection in the water, folio 78v.

Page 31: The hawk and the chicken converse, folio 80r.

Page 32: The gardener digs for treasure, folio 82r.

Page 35: The leopard attacks the hunter, folio 84r.

Page 36: The lion watches the crow, the wolf, and the jackal eat the dead camel, folio 87r.

Page 39: The geese carry the tortoise over a village, folio 89v.

Page 41: The phoenix and his army of birds, folio 91r.

Page 43: The King of Lions attacks Shanzabeh, folio 92r.

Page 44: Monkeys pluck the bird while a man watches, folio 95r.

Page 47: The frog, the crab, and the snake, folio 97r.

Page 48: The judge and Sharp-Wit next to the burning tree, folio 98v.

Page 50: The bear kills the
gardener with a stone,
folio 102r.

Page 52: The bird flies off with
the piece of skin, folio 107v.

Page 55: The King of Lions, his
mother, and the court, folio 113r.

Page 56: The sheikh saves the holy
man from execution, folio 118v.

Page 59: Kalilah visits Dimnah
in prison, folio 126r.

For my grandson, Ilias Habíb Daoud

First published in Canada in 2013 by
The Aga Khan Museum
Toronto, Ontario, Canada
www.agakhanmuseum.org

Series Editor: Ruba Kana'an
Editor: Michael Carroll
Design: Ingrid Paulson

Jacket and Cover Illustrations:
Anwar-i Suhayli (*Lights of Canopus*)
Rendered into Persian by Husayn ibn 'Ali al-Wa'iz al-Kashifi
Illustrations attributed to Sadiqi Beg
Qazvin, Iran, 1593
Opaque watercolour, gold, ink, paper
AKM289

Front Jacket and Cover Illustration: Shanzabeh and Dimnah before the King of Lions, folio 55r.

5 4 3 2 1   17 16 15 14 13

LIBRARY AND ARCHIVES CANADA CATALOGUING IN PUBLICATION

Laird, Elizabeth, 1943–, author
Two crafty jackals : the animal fables of Kalilah and Dimnah / Elizabeth Laird;
illustrations attributed to Sadiqi Beg.

ISBN 978-0-9919928-1-2 (bound)

I. Sadig bāǐ Ǎfshar, 1533–, illustrator II. Title.

PZ7.LI579 Two 2013   j823'.92   C2013-903524-9

Printed and bound in China

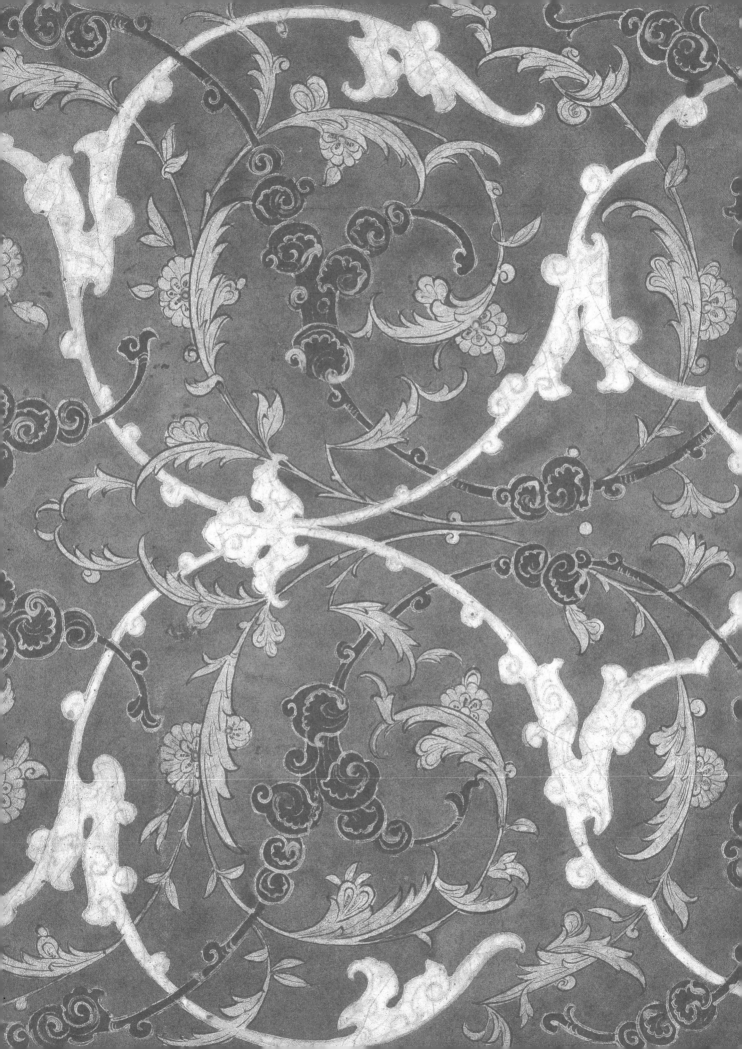